Maisie's Merry Christmas

Maisie's Merry Christmas

Author and illustrator Aileen Paterson

THE AMAISING PUBLISHING HOUSE LTD

This book is dedicated to my grandchildren

with thanks to Mark Blackadder

GLOSSARY

BY JINGS	BEIJING — Capital of China
Toerag	ruffian or rascal
in a tizzy	agitated
in a huff	sulking
ticky-wee	tiny
sherbet dabs	lollipops to dip in sherbet
you look a ticket	you're a mess

© Aileen Paterson

First published in 1995 by The Amaising Publishing House Ltd, reprinted 1996, 1997.

This edition published in 1999 by:
Glowworm Books Ltd, Unit 7, Greendykes Industrial Estate,
Broxburn, West Lothian, EH52 6PG, Scotland.

Telephone: 01506-857570
Fax: 01506-858100
E-mail: admin@glowwormbooks.co.uk
URL: http://www.glowwormbooks.co.uk

ISBN 1 871512 46 8

Printed and bound by Scotprint, Musselburgh.

Designed by Mark Blackadder.

Reprint Code   10   9   8   7   6   5   4

Other Maisie titles in the Series:

Maisie and the Space Invader
Maisie's Festival Adventure
Maisie goes to Hospital
What Maisie did Next
Maisie and the Puffer
Maisie digs up the Past

Maisie and the Posties
Maisie and the Pirates
Maisie in the Rainforest
Maisie goes to Hollywood
Maisie loves Paris
Maisie goes to School

Christmas comes but once a year, they say, but it begins to sneak up on you long before December . .

"What did you paint today?" Maisie asked Archie as they walked home from school one afternoon.

"A big pepperoni pizza."

"A PIZZA? I thought we were supposed to paint our favourite animal."

"I know," laughed Archie, "but I was feeling hungry."

"I painted an elephant to send to my Daddy. He's away exploring in a place called By Jings."

"BY JINGS! Where's that?"

"I think it's the capital of China," said Maisie. "Daddy says there's a lot to explore there. He's going to see pandas and a big wall and sail up a yellow river. He won't be home for a long time, not until Christmas."

"Never mind," said Archie taking her paw. "Come on, let's race to the corner."

When Maisie arrived home she found Granny in the kitchen with their pernickety neighbour, Mrs McKitty.

"Hello everybody, I'm home," cried Maisie.

"Hello my wee lamb," smiled Granny.

"Hello Maisie," cried Mrs McKitty. "My, what a ticket you look. Were you blown in by a hurricane?"

"No," laughed Maisie, "but I've been running up the stairs to find out what Granny's cooking. What's that nice spicy smell?"

"I've been baking," said Granny. "Christmas cakes."

"Christmas cakes already! But Granny, we've just had Hallowe'en."

"I know Maisie, but the longer you keep Christmas cake, the better it tastes. Anyway, Christmas will be here sooner than you think. Every year its the same — one mad rush!"

"Absolutely," agreed Mrs McKitty. "It's beginning already. I'm the secretary of The Morningside Operacatic Society, and the committee are coming to my flat this evening. We must plan what show we're doing for Christmas."

"What's a committee?" asked Maisie.

"Clever cats like me who get picked to get things done. Our meeting won't take long, mind you.

I've decided that we should do 'The Sound of Mewsic'. I'll be perfect for the heroine!"

Goodness me, thought Maisie. Christmas cakes and Christmas meetings. Why is it that big cats think Christmas is just around the corner, and wee kittens know it won't be here for AGES . . .

That evening, when Maisie was tucked up in bed and Granny
was knitting by the fire, Mrs McKitty's meeting began.
All the committee were there. Mr Havers, Mr MacStoorie,
Miss Gingersnapp, Mrs Finnan-Haddie and Mrs McKitty, of course.
She fetched in coffee for everyone.

"Can I press you to a pancake?" she asked. "Or perhaps a rock
cake? Take your pick."

After coffee it was time to plan their Christmas show.

Mrs McKitty was flabbergasted when the meeting didn't go as she had planned. NO ONE wanted to do 'The Sound of Mewsic'!

Instead, they all voted for a Pantomime — including Mrs McKitty's budgie, Billy, and he wasn't even a member. She was very annoyed with Billy, and even more annoyed when he piped up with some more bright ideas.

"Cinderella! Cinderella!" he squawked. "Cinderella is the bees knees. With Maisie and Archie in it!"

"What a splendid idea," meowed Miss Gingersnapp.

"Maisie MacKenzie would make a lovely Cinderella, and Archie can be her prince. Well done Billy!"

"Who's a clever budgie?" chirped Billy.

Everyone voted for Billy's ideas . . . except Mrs McKitty.

She was in The Huff! She wanted nothing to do with this feather brained nonsense. Clever budgie indeed! Then Mr MacStoorie came up with a plan which changed her mind completely. He said that Mrs McKitty was the very cat to run the show.

Suddenly Mrs McKitty LOVED the whole idea. A Christmas Pantomime with kittens in it . . . WONDERFUL! . . . and Marjorie Millicent McKitty in charge.

She began making a list right away!

moi?

When Maisie awoke next morning she had no idea that Christmas was beginning to sneak up on her. It seemed like an ordinary Saturday, tidying up and shopping, until Mrs McKitty arrived.

"ME! Cinderella in a PANTOMIME? But, but, but . . ." gasped Maisie, amazed at Mrs McKitty's news. Granny was delighted, and said it was a great idea — until she heard the next bit of news. Mrs McKitty wanted her to be The Fairy Godmother AND make all the costumes!

"But, but, but . . ." stammered Granny, but Mrs McKitty had no time for BUTS. She had already left and was off to tell all the other cats and kittens what parts they would play.

"Me a prince? But, Mrs McKitty . . . " cried Archie. Too late. Mrs McKitty had swept into the flat next door to see the MacTuff brothers . . . and when she announced that the rough-tough MacTuffs (a pair of toerags she usually called them) were going to play The Ugly SISTERS and wear frilly frocks — they fainted!

Soon Mrs McKitty had ticked off everyone and everything on her list . . . except for one little problem . . . THE MICE.

Mrs McKitty didn't know any mice. "There are no mice in *MORNINGSIDE,* as you know," she cried, "and we need six for my pantomime."

"Yes there are!" said Maisie. "They live down by the railway line. I'll go and see them tomorrow. I'm sure they would love to help us."

Mr and Mrs Mouse were quite surprised when Maisie rang their doorbell and peeked into their mousehole. (They didn't get many pussycat visitors.)

Maisie was very polite and explained all about the pantomime.

She spoke very quietly in case she frightened the mouse babies. (Goodness Gracious there were lots of them!)

"Very well," said Mr Mouse. "We agree. We will come along with our friends, The Von Trapps, to the first rehearsal. Here is our phone number Maisie, in case you need to give us a ring."

As soon as work began on the pantomime Christmas seemed to draw nearer and nearer, bringing a magic tingle . . . and LOTS of hard work.

Every night the orchestra practiced their music.

Every night, after she had done her homework, Maisie had to learn her lines so she would not forget any of them.

Every night Mrs McKitty got into a tizzy twenty times.

Every night Granny had to sew the costumes, even the ticky-wee clothes for the mice.

Every night somebody got cross!

But one day the posters for the pantomime were ready, and everyone felt pleased when they saw them in the shops and in the library. All the cats in Morningside were buying tickets for their Christmas show.

Maisie was so busy she almost forgot to send her letter to Santa Claws. It was only one week before Christmas when she sat down to write a long letter telling him all her news . . .

Far away in his workshop near the North Pole, Santa was very busy too. He was up to his ears and whiskers in work, and wondering if he would be ready on time. During his tea break he opened the last of his letters.

"Jumping Jinglebells, what a treat," he cried. "A letter from MAISIE! I feel better already. Let's see what she's up to . . ."

This is what he read. . .

Dear Santa,

I hope you and the reindeer are well and don't have the cold. It's freezing here in Edinburgh but I'm fine and so is Granny. We've got Supercat hot water bottles. Daddy is home AT LAST! He came last night when I was in my jammies. He's been in Paris to give a talk to the Parisites, and then on an expedition to China. He's been very busy exploring and visiting the pandas. He said it was Pandamonium!

I've got exciting news. I'm going to be Cinderella in a pantomime! I wish you could come and see it. Granny is my Fairy Granny, Archie is the prince and Mrs McKitty is my wicked stepmother, Mrs Bossyboots. Guess what — The MacTuff brothers are the Ugly Sisters, Plooketta and Scabina. The mice are in it too. Mrs McKitty gave them a ticking-off for squeaking during rehearsal. She said, "One more TOOT, and you're OOT!" The mice got cross and went on strike, but it's alright now. Granny made them a cheesecake.

I've got butterflies in my tummy. It's scary being Cinderella in a big theatre. Christmas is coming very quickly this year, just like Granny said it would. I hope we'll all be ready in time.

We've got to learn our words!
We've got to write our Christmas cards!
We've got to do our Christmas Shopping!
We've got to post our parcels!

Granny's all of a twitter and Mrs McKitty's all of a doodah. It's one mad rush here in Morningside.

Lots of love.

Maisie xxxxxx

P.S. I forgot to ask you if I could please have some storybooks and a watch with Supercat on it? Thank you.

"Dearie me," smiled Santa when he'd finished reading the letter. "Maisie's just as busy as me this year. A pantomime too. My, I wish I could see that. I've never been to a pantomime. I'm always too busy before Christmas, and after Christmas I just come home and heat up some soup, then sleep till Eastertime. Ah well, I'd better get back to work. I've one-hundred-and-one things to do. I'll need to wrap Maisie's presents too. She'll be a grand wee Cinderella."

Things that must be done, the Noo!
glueing. (fix central heating)
packing.
wrapping.
counting
* checking
weather forecast
* tonic for reindeer
* wash the dishes
buy milk

Aileen Paterson '95

By the time Maisie's letter reached Santa Claws Maisie was beginning to feel she wouldn't be a grand Cinderella at all. It was the First Night of the pantomime! Daddy was very excited as he took his seat in the front row. The audience were happily waiting for the curtains to open. Behind the curtain, the kittens all felt like running away as fast as they could. They were so nervous. But when the curtain opened, and everyone clapped, a strange thing happened . . . they began to enjoy themselves!

Even the MacTuff brothers loved it when
the audience giggled as they appeared in their
frilly frocks and began to speak . . .

"Cinderella! Do your stuff,
We have waited long enough.
Hurry up and make the tea,
Mince and Tatties NOW for three."

And the audience burst out laughing
when they got dressed to go to the Palace,
and Mrs McKitty did her bit as Mrs Bossyboots.

"Come along or we'll be late,
The 23 bus doesn't wait.
I'll be the smartest at the Ball,
And you two, fairest of them all."

THE PANTOMIME WAS A HIT!

On the second night the kittens enjoyed every moment,
and the audience did too.
They clapped and clapped when Granny appeared
with her magic wand and helped Cinderella . . .

"Hello Cinders, do not fear,
Now your Fairy Granny's here.
Before you can wink, or jump in the sink,
You'll be a picture in yellow and pink!"

They gasped when the pumpkin changed into a coach
and the mice changed into ponies and servants . . .
and Maisie had a beautiful ball dress . . .

"I've never seen such magic stuff,
And shoes of GLASS in all my puff.
Fairy Granny, thanks to you,
You have made my dreams come true."

And everyone sighed when, at the end, Maisie tried on
the glass slipper and it FITTED!

Never had there been such a pantomime. Mrs McKitty, the Director, got lots of claps and bunches of flowers, and her photograph in 'The Scotscat' and 'The Morningside Tattler'! What a feather in her cap!

The last night of the pantomime was on Christmas Eve.

What a surprise for Maisie and the mice when the curtains opened.

Santa Claws was sitting in the front row next to Daddy, eating sherbet dabs and clapping his paws! ! !

Maisie told Archie about it whilst they were dancing. Santa had a great time seeing his first pantomime, just before he began the long journey to deliver his presents.

When the pantomime ended, and the audience had gone home to hang up their stockings, he went backstage to thank everyone.

He had a special treat for Maisie and Archie . . . that night, all of the magic of Christmas arrived when Santa Claws took them home. They flew across the night sky — zooming in the sleigh over Edinburgh Castle, which lay below sparkling in the frosty air. Later that night when the kittens were asleep in their beds, Santa delivered their presents . . .

The Morningside mice weren't forgotten on Christmas Eve.
Father Krismouse visited the mouse house . . .
. . . and Billy the budgie wasn't forgotten either . . .

On Christmas Day Maisie had her merriest Christmas EVER.
Instead of going home to heat up some soup, Santa came to her
house for dinner. Just before Granny served up the turkey and
tatties, there was a surprise for him. For the first time ever, there
were Christmas presents for Santa, and his very own Christmas
cake.

All the rush was over. There was peace and joy
everywhere . . . and it happens just like this every year.